The Shepherdess

The Story of St. Germaine Cousin

Andie Andrews

Flying
Chestnut
Press

Author's Note: This book was inspired by the brief life of St. Germaine Cousin of Pibrac as illuminated by Catholic history and tradition. Some names, characters, details, and events have been novelized as a means of presenting her story with heart and imagination while remaining faithful to the essence of her biography and heroic journey to sainthood.

Published by Flying Chestnut Press

ISBN 979-8-9858456-2-4

To my beloved mother, Dorothy,
who was born on June 15th,
the Feast of St. Germaine.

Prologue

H er sudden appearance was an act of mercy. For what other *raison d'être* would this saintly girl fly to my deathbed as the infant at my grossly deformed breast grasped for milk and gasped for air, even as I cried out in despair with my own last breaths? I knew her, even before she opened her dainty mouth to speak, for I had seen her in the tomb.

"Hush, dear Marié," she whispered sweetly as she nestled a velvet stool against my tufted mattress. She perched upon it like a delicate goldfinch, her shimmering, yellow tresses draping her pathetically thin shoulders like downy wings. "The prayers of your husband, François, have reached my ears and I, in turn, have begged the tender compassion of our God."

"Germaine!" I moaned, as she grasped my hand.

The peasant girl whose name I had slandered, whose memory I had sought to banish, whose incorrupt body I had relegated to the darkest corner of the sacristy, had come bearing light. It bathed the angular features of her unblemished face, brushed the bones of her sunken cheeks, and pierced her dewy, grey eyes like the sun pierces the

morning mist that settles in these sleepy lowlands nine miles outside
the grand city of Toulouse.

It is this same grandness that has been my downfall. I had threatened to withdraw my most generous alms from the coffers of the
church if the village priest refused to remove the offensive corpse of
"the holy shepherdess" from my sight. So near was it to my pew that I
could scarcely think of anything but death. Her death and my own!
This poor, suffering saint of Pibrac, Germaine Cousin, had passed
away forty-three years ago, in 1601, at the age of twenty-two. I was
but three years older than she had been at the time of her demise. Her
tomb was a grotesque reminder that if it could happen to her, it could
happen to me. To my dear François, my guardian and my love. And to
my precious, newborn son, René, who whimpered in my arms, unable
to nurse. What I had feared and detested most — an indiscriminate
death — had abruptly come to call. In desperation, I had sent François
to the church to summon the mercy of God through the intercession
of the girl behind the glass.

And now, here she was.

Her mere presence lifted the pall. My pain began to subside. My
baby slept. Germaine squeezed my hand and began to speak tenderly.
I now see that in that shining moment, she had come to shepherd me,
a proud and prodigal daughter, a willful and wayward lamb, back into
the fold of God's love.

This is her story, as she told it to me.

1

That I am able to hold your hand, dear Marié, with my own right hand is a testament to the full restoration that awaits us in heaven. See? There is no more atrophy to curl my calloused palm and hinder the use of my right arm, which once hung uselessly at my side. My fingers are straight and pleasant to behold, no longer subject to the cruel taunts of the children of Pibrac and my own half-siblings. To be born with such deformities might have been found worthy of pity, but to also have been stricken as a young child with the disease of scrofula, which horribly disfigured my face and neck, made me an outcast and contemptible to all. Even to my own father.

My father! I am told that Laurent Cousin had once been held in high esteem. His own father had been a tailor by trade and became the much beloved mayor of the village of Pibrac. His keen sense of economy and industry enabled him to purchase a handsome tract of land in the countryside that my father came to inherit. The farm was rich in pastureland, bordered by stands of sweet chestnut trees to the east and the deep, wild Forest of Bouconne to the west. It was on that very farm that I was born and that my mother died a mere six months after giving birth to me. I like to think that she loved and cherished me despite the fact that my right hand was gnarled and I was said to be weak in constitution from the start. I know little of my early survival and even less about my mother's manner of death though I suspect it was from the plague. My father never spoke of it, or of her, and paid me little attention. To the farm, he paid even less, keeping but a flock of sheep, a couple of dairy cows, and a few crops in the ground to sustain us and the procession of nannies who came and went in his employ. I can barely remember any one of them, and their indiscriminate care left me vulnerable to all kinds of ailments. Hence, it was no surprise to anyone in the village when I began, at the age of five, to show the first signs of scrofula, an ulcerative disease for which there was said to be no cure, save the touch of a sovereign king. Just a few months before my medical diagnosis, my father had met and married Hortense, a stout, shrewish woman from Toulouse who arrived at our farmhouse, sight unseen, with her own two daughters in tow. I think she despised me from the moment she saw me.

"So this is Germaine," she pronounced, eyeing me from the top of my tangled hair to my dirty, unshod feet. I didn't even own a pair of shoes but I didn't care. I didn't need them. I never left the farm, not even for Mass on Sundays, though my father would occasionally attend without me. Even then, I remember longing to hasten toward the sound of the bells. But they were never meant for me. My Sundays were spent ambling in the pastures in communion with nature, which I understood to be a sign of something — or someone— much, much grander.

"Say hello to your new mother," my father coaxed. New mother? I didn't know if I should be delighted or despair, for I'd never really been mothered before and didn't know what to expect. "And to your new sisters, Jacqueline and Abigail. Abby is your age, Germaine, why don't you show her the fancy new doll I brought you from Toulouse?"

Even at that tender age, a sense of injustice reared. My father had just bought me my first and only French porcelain doll the week before bringing Hortense to the farm. It was blond and fair and lovely, and finely dressed in brocade and silk. Did he really expect me to share the only toy he had ever given me? But share I would, for he glanced at me sternly and I turned my head aside in shame.

"What's that on the side of her neck?" Hortense sneered.

"What do you mean?" my father replied as he pulled my blond hair away from my nape. It hurt, and I grimaced.

"She's blotchy. And rough skinned. It looks — unseemly," she said, her pudgy nose turning upward as she fussed with her elegant chignon.

"She likely got into something outside. I'm afraid she runs with the wind. Perhaps your daughters can teach her a more, shall we say, genteel manner of play?"

Hortense rolled her narrow brown eyes and shrugged. "Go along, girls."

Abigail and Jacqueline, who were as rotund and squinty-eyed as their mother, held their ground.

"I said, go on!" Hortense repeated, this time with a low growl. The girls flinched and looked to me for a clue.

"Come with me, " I exclaimed, grabbing Abigail's wrist with my able left hand. "I'll show you my doll, her name is Celeste. She has bright blue eyes that blink!"

"How can she even play with a doll with one hand?" Jacqueline mused with a rude little laugh. I was so happy to have siblings that I glossed over the insult.

"You need to keep an eye on that neck of hers," Hortense muttered to my father. "With all the plagues and indignities among us, we can't risk her falling ill, it could be the death of us all."

"Yes, dear. I promise such things shall never come to pass. Not on my watch. Never again."

"Good," Hortense huffed. And that was the last I heard before I skipped from the room.

2

Within a couple of months, the cluster of purplish, raised blotches on the right side of my neck began to spread to my face, marring chin, my cheek, and reaching nearly to my temple. They didn't hurt, nor did they itch like the poison ivy rash I'd contracted once before. By this time, both Hortense and my stepsisters shrank from my presence, while my father continued the benign neglect to which I was accustomed. Jacqueline and Abigail snickered and made monstrous sounds whenever I came into view, and Hortense began to leave meager meals for me on the outside steps as though I were some sort of feral cat. When, six months later, the blotches began to abscess and spread toward my mouth, making it difficult for me to eat, my father called Dr. Marmét, from Toulouse, to come and have a look at me.

"Scrofula," he pronounced with a heavy sigh. "The king's evil. There's no cure for it save the touch of a king."

"Then we shall go to see the King, shall we not, Papa?" I chirped.

"We haven't the means for that," my father snapped. He refused to look at me, preferring to drum his long, slender fingers on the kitchen table as he glanced nervously around the room, fearing Hortense's return from town. She'd left early that morning for the dressmaker's shop to commission new frocks for herself and her daughters for *Dimanche de Pâques*, the great solemnity of the Lord's Resurrection. More likely than not, I would be left to wear the same ragged dress that currently draped my small, bony body, it's once gay, pink color faded to the color of a pale bruise. I had practically outgrown it but dared to hope I might at least receive one of my stepsisters' hand-me-downs!

"What then," my father asked the good doctor, "shall we do to — help Germaine?"

Dr. Marmét gazed at me with a deep compassion in his eyes that I will never forget.

"Treat her kindly. Make her days memorable. And hope and pray for the best. The Lord is merciful. Perhaps he will perform a miracle." With that, he grabbed his black bag and headed for the door.

"Wait!" my father called out. "What shall I tell my wife? Is she contagious?"

The doctor paused at the threshold and shrugged. "Time will tell, but I expect her overall, weak constitution contributed to her infection. I wouldn't be too worried. The well-nourished seldom get sick. Germaine is pathetically thin. Give her something to eat."

As the dilapidated door shuddered behind him, a crisp, spring breeze snuck into the kitchen.

"The fresh air will do you good," my father said with a trace of sorrow and a somber shake of his head. Still, he refused to look me in the eyes. Since I had not inherited his deep blue eyes, I could only surmise that I had inherited my mother's grey ones. He could not see me without seeing her. "Run along and play. Perhaps there are newborn lambs in the barn, why don't you go and see?"

"Oh!" I squealed with delight. "Yes, Eleanora looked more than ready when I saw her yesterday. I think I should bring her a handful of extra oats, don't you think so, Papa?"

"That sounds like a good idea, *ma chérie*. And take a big slice of Hortense's freshly baked bread with some butter on it for yourself." He gazed down at the table, scrunched his bulbous nose, and fumbled with the shiny wedding band on his left hand. He looked like he might cry.

My own eyes brimmed with tears. My father had never spoken a single term of endearment to me, not in my six years on earth. Nor had he ever been solicitous of my health or nutrition. I thought perhaps my affliction was meant to be a blessing that would draw us closer, into the natural order of love between parent and child. Little did I know that it would be the *coupe de grâce* that would end my life as I knew it.

From that day on, I was no longer welcome in my own house. My diagnosis was ill-received by Hortense, whose shrill insults regularly reached my ears in the nearby barn where I had been commanded to stay until either my affliction — or I — had passed.

"I'll not subject my beautiful girls to her hideous condition. Look at her, Laurent, she's an embarrassment to the House of Cousin. And a danger to society, if you ask me. There's no sense in educating her, so why not send her into the fields to care for the sheep? She can sleep out there for all I care."

"Hortense, for the love of God, show some mercy. There are wolves and wild beasts in *La Bouccone*. She's but a lamb herself. They could just as easily carry her off in the dark of night and tear her to pieces!"

"And your point?" Hortese scoffed.

In the silence that followed, I prayed to a God I barely knew. I prayed to my unknown mother too.

"At least let her sleep in the barn with the sheep. And provide some decent morsels of food for her each day," my father bargained.

"Fine," Hortense retorted. "But if I see her anywhere near this house, I'll chase her off with a broom — or worse!"

I had never seen the point in telling my father that Hortese had already struck me more than once with the kitchen broom, as well as with the back of her hand, since her arrival on the farm. To add to the insult, her impressionable daughters often sprinkled ashes on my food, which was set on a small plate beside the dog's dish on the back porch. If they thought it would render my bread inedible, they were wrong. I had taken to eating bark and chestnuts and certain seasonal flowers in the field as hunger dictated. A few ashes would not deter me. What I did long for was fresh, clean clothing so that I might one day be fit to appear at Mass on Sundays. My stepsisters occasionally left me pieces of used clothing, though Jacqueline mockingly coated hers with pitch from the trees, making them sticky and unwearable. In some ways, I was glad for my increasingly ugly appearance, for it now deterred my step-siblings from getting close enough to bully me. Given my disabilities, I could hardly defend myself from their blows. I found that out the day that Jacqueline pushed me to the ground, pummeled my head, and stole my dear Celeste for her own, despite my attempts to clutch my prized doll with my left arm. As battered as I had been, I couldn't really blame my stepsisters for their behavior. It was learned from their mother, whose sin dripped from her tongue and oozed out of her corpulent body and infected those around her more deeply — and mortally — than my own disease ever could.

The barn to which I'd been banished was broad and tall, with rafters that hosted all kinds of birds and other creatures. I was particularly fond of the barn owl, who didn't seem to mind that I had taken up residence below. Her creamy feathers framed a pale white face dotted with gleaming black eyes that regarded me with what I perceived to be solicitude and warmth. I didn't have to fear that mice or other rodents would crawl about me as I slept, for her keen appetite kept them at bay. Except for the sheep, I refrained from giving my barn companions names. They were wild and free and beyond human conventions. I simply called her Owl.

Among the first tasks I undertook was to make a mattress of sorts for myself, choosing to tuck it into a small cavity under the stairs leading to the hay loft. I had roamed the pastures at liberty for the first few years of my life and knew where to find soft, pliable vines that would nestle my body. With great difficulty owing to my infirmities, I wove the vines between some strong twigs for support, topped the mattress with straw for loft and warmth, and set it atop a wooden pallet to suspend me off the damp, dirt floor. I was pleased with my rough-hewn bed. And the castaway clothing that Jacquline had coated with pitch? I collected several pieces from a pile and turned them inside out, knotting them together to form a thin blanket for myself. Even then, what one intended for evil, God had turned to the good!

My vine-twig bed beneath the stairs was sheltered from the drafts that seeped through the barn boards yet positioned to allow the morning sun to stream through one of the upper windows and flood it with light. Thus the sun, and the resident barnyard rooster, ensured that I awakened at dawn to collect my meager portion of bread from the back porch of the house before driving my flock of sheep to the near pasture for the day. If I was lucky, I was able to avoid seeing Hortense, but on those mornings when I did, she would curl her lip in disdain and salt my bread with insult. Over time, I learned the exact measure of a broom handle and the cudgel she kept by the back door. If I kept a proper distance, no harm would come to me. There were, however, some days when a meanness in Hortense would prevail, and I would end up sorely bruised just the same.

One day, she met me at the back door with a spindle and distaff in her hands. She ordered me to stand back and pay attention as she demonstrated how to use the tools to spin wool. I was confused by the whole affair. After all, how could I, with but one functional hand, ever hope to spin anything at all? When she finished her demonstration, she tossed the instruments at my feet.

"You're nearly seven years old, Germaine. It's time you earn your keep. If you want your bread in the morning I'll expect to see bundles of thread by my door this evening. Put your day's labor in here," she said, motioning to a basket at her feet that was filled with shorn wool. "You'll receive your bread accordingly."

I went hungry for nearly a week. Eventually I figured out how to load and hold the distaff, twist the fiber, and gather it onto the drop spindle with one able hand and a half-useless one. But the more I practiced and adapted, the more proficient I became until I considered myself not only a shepherdess but a spinner as well. Before long, Hortense restored my former ration of bread, though there was never a morsel more, no matter how much spun wool I produced.

There was a comforting rhythm to my days at pasture with my flock of twenty sheep. While I wasn't much bigger than they were, and most certainly weighed less, they sensed my concern for their well-being and allowed me to inspect or doctor them as needed. This included spring and early summer lambing, when one ewe or another would wander off on her own in search of a quiet and protected place to lie down and give birth. As I spun my wool, I'd watch the pregnant ewes paw at the tender earth to create a nest of sorts for themselves and then sink into it, their breath becoming more labored by the minute. Most times, within the hour or so, the ewe would stand up to nurse her newborn lamb or even twin lambs. Occasionally, when one labored too long, I'd have to intervene and help to right the head or shoulders of a lamb coming through the birth canal. Over the years, I looked into many the eye of a ewe in distress, begging my help to save her and the life of her lamb. When a lamb or ewe succumbed to death despite my efforts, I buried them with dignity and simple invocations I composed myself, not being formally schooled in the way of prayer.

That's how I met Pierre. He was my first real friend, a local beggar who occasionally earned a few coins as a hired hand on nearby farms, but more often than not, owing to the fragility of his mind and a tendency to twitch and blurt, languished under one of the sweet chestnut trees, biding his time until sunset each day. The first ewe I ever lost to lambing, my precious Odette, made me drop to my knees in sorrow, my thin, childish wails reaching his ears. He wandered near and I felt him peering at my hunched back as it rose and fell with uncontrolled sobs.

"You did the best you could for her," he consoled me from several steps away. I was a mere seven years old. I did not want him to draw any closer as I was unused to the tone he used with me. It sounded gentle in my ears but I couldn't trust his intentions. I trusted no one to care for me, sick as I was. And certainly not a stranger.

"Don't come any closer," I called out. "I'm...*unwell*."

"So am I," he replied.

"She was my one of my favorite ewes," I stammered between soft hiccups of grief.

"I know. I'm very sorry. Allow me to take the body and deposit it in the forest for you."

I gasped and lifted my head from the ground. "She deserves a better ending than that!"

Pierre nodded his head slowly. It was the first time I noticed how young he actually was, likely not more than his mid-twenties. Hardship had etched deep furrows on his forehead and his face was pale and drawn, but there was a kindness in his light blue eyes that took offense at nothing, least of all my petulant reply.

"It is like saying that just because we're sickly, or our lives have ended, we ought to be thrown to the wolves!" I protested. I believe in that moment, I spoke for both of us in a way that only makes sense to the poor and marginalized.

"I promise you, I'll give her a proper burial." Pierre smiled softly. The sight of his smile startled me at first, but then brought about an enormous sense of relief and confidence that all would be well for Odette. I stopped crying as he scooped my precious, white ewe into in his lanky arms and carried her toward the dark silhouette of pine trees that marked the boundary of *La Bouconne*. I don't know where he buried her, or how he came by the means to do so. I only know that a deep friendship was forged in that field of tears and trials. Clearly he had his own, and yet he showed me from an early age that it is possible to smile through adversity, if not for our own sake, but for the benefit of those who seek Christ in our faces.

I supposed that losing Odette in the struggle to give life also released a floodgate of guilt and sorrow I felt over the loss of my own mother. While no one outrightly blamed me for her death, I had always wondered if the sight of me, a weak, deformed baby girl, had so disappointed her that she gradually lost her own brightness and vigor. Or, perhaps, she had made some kind of bargain with God — that is, made a sacrificial lamb of herself in exchange for my life and happiness. As a mother of sorts to my flock, a shepherdess of their very lives, I felt that I would do anything to spare them pain or suffering if I could. I was told by the nanny who cared for me just before Hortense arrived that there is a Good Shepherd who reigns above and watches over His flock; that I am a little lamb who is much beloved by Him. She said I should accompany my father to church if I wanted to get to know this Good Shepherd. I resolved there and then to ask my father if I could attend Mass on Sundays, even if I wasn't allowed to sit with my family. The pasturing of the sheep would only be delayed a short time. I hoped he would not withhold his consent on account of my stepmother's embarrassment over me. I had stifled my heart's desire long enough!

That night, when I returned my day's labor of spun wool to the basket, I knocked loudly on the back door of the house. It was so dusky that the whole world appeared cloaked in blue shadows and I lowered the frayed hood of my cape as the flimsy, wooden door swung open.

"What do you want?" Jacqueline snapped.

"I'd like to see my father."

"He's at table."

"Please, tell him I'd like a word with him, it won't take but a minute."

Jacqueline heaved a sigh and nonchalantly closed the door. She eyed me cautiously through the gaping boards and I felt like a wild beast in a crate. Even then, a little voice inside me said that she was the one held captive, not me. I knew the freedom of the broad, green earth, while she was stuck inside, in the clutches of her mother's envy and hate.

"Jacqueline! Please!"

She didn't say another word before she scurried off. I had no real hope that my father would appear, or that he would even be told I was at the door. I thought I heard a brief squabble coming from within. Seconds later, my father appeared. He arched a bushy eyebrow as he scanned my face and neck, perhaps seeking signs of improvement. Seeing none, he grimaced and spoke in a hushed voice.

"What is it, Germaine?"

I longed to ask him a dozen questions. *Are you well, Papa? Are you happy? Do you ever think about maman like I do? Do you like being married again? Have you come to love Jacqueline and Abigail? I do not think I am contagious, may I come back into the house? Did you know Hortense beats me every chance she gets? Why do I go hungry, Papa? Have a been a bad girl? Do I disgust you? Why don't you defend me? Papa, do you love me?*

"I'd like your permission to attend Mass on Sunday."

"That would take you away from the pasture for quite some time," my father said with a shake of his head. "Who would care for the sheep?"

"It would only be one day a week, Papa. How will I grow up to be a good and holy person if I am prevented from learning how? The sheep will not suffer for so short a time."

My father tilted his head and scratched at the scruff of his evening beard. His dark blue eyes squinted with indecision.

"Please, Papa, I won't be a bother to you or to Hortense. I won't travel or sit with you, I'll be as quiet as a dormouse in the back of the church!" I pleaded.

"The Courbet runs high after it rains, Germaine. It can be too risky to cross."

"It's mostly a pleasant stream or a dry bed, I won't cross it if it's too high." I smiled and nodded, hoping to win his favor. "All I ask is that you tell the priest that I'm permitted to attend — and tell your new family too," I added, wanting to spare myself a beating.

"Laurent, your food is getting cold!" Hortense screeched from the dining room. "I've labored over hot coals to produce a nice meal for you, the least you can do is come and eat it."

"One moment, *mon amour!*" my father cried out, then reverted to a whisper. "You have my permission. I will speak to Father Michel about the matter. But you must do your part and keep to yourself. I'm afraid there's no place for you in the pew with Hortense and the girls."

I knew that also meant there was no place for me beside my father. But I was pleased to obtain his consent just the same.

"Thank you, Papa!" I quietly exclaimed. I deliberately stepped backward to prevent myself from running into his arms.

"God be with you, Germaine."

I took my father's blessing and held it to my heart, even as he shut the door in my face. I hoped his words would prove true, that the God I already sensed in the vast, blue canopy of sky, the bounties of the earth, and the joy I felt in the company of my flock, would indeed be with me in new and wondrous ways. Oh, my little soul was filled with anticipation as I skipped to the barn, the hunger in my belly replaced by a new and mysterious hunger that would turn out to be greater than any I had ever known!

3

The following Sunday, I awoke before dawn and lingered on my pallet-bed beneath the stairs longer than usual. On typical, early spring days, I would eagerly wrap myself in the rough blanket my father had mercifully provided over the winter and waddle to the threshold to watch the sun slowly rise above the gangly, bare limbs of the sweet chestnut trees. Soon, they would be adorned with a covering of dark green, serrated leaves that would prevent me from seeing the eastern horizon. But this time of year, I could bathe myself in a fresh golden light that made me feel clean and pretty despite the ulcers on my face and the poverty of my dress. That morning, however, I was reluctant to rise. I did not feel clean or pretty and no amount of sunlight could make me so. How could I dare to appear in church, the very house of God, in my pitiful condition? I began to weep as I picked shards of straw from my rumpled, pale pink frock. Eleanor, the grand ewe of my flock, drew nearer at the sound and before long, I was encircled by my little bastion of sheep. They not only knew my voice. They knew my cries and encamped around me like an army of woolen angels. I ran the fingers of my able hand through the wavy fleece covering Eleanor's long, graceful neck and she nuzzled my shoulder with a sweetness that brought me comfort and strength. Like them, I was delicate in body and bone and vulnerable to predators of every sort, human and animal alike. And yet, despite their inability to defend themselves, they faced each new day with courage and a singularity of purpose: to simply be as God created them. I was created deformed and bedeviled by disease. But my heart, like theirs, was pure. This thought inspired me to focus on what lies within and I stopped picking vainly at my threadbare clothing. I set my feet on the cold, earthen floor and arose from my bed with a vaporous puff of newfound courage. God himself would provide what I needed that day, just as he provided peaceful pastures for my flock and sweet, long grasses in their mouths.

Having believed it would be so, I was not surprised to find a package wrapped in brown paper at the threshold of the barn. I glanced cautiously into the shifting shadows of dawn. Seeing nothing and no one, I picked up the package and stared at it, hardly knowing what to do next. No one had ever given me a present wrapped with a bow before. I returned to my straw mattress and sat down, fingering the pink satin ribbon for a very long time. As the first strands of golden light streamed through the upper window, I released the bow and peeled back the flaps of paper. There, folded into a neat square, was a pristine, linen dress, the vibrant, sky-blue color of the posies that grow along the banks of the Courbet, commonly known as forget-me-nots. Knowing in my heart that it was a gift from my dear Papa, I couldn't help but wonder if the dress itself was imbued with a deeper meaning. Perhaps my father, for all his neglect, had not forgotten me!

I resolved to make it my Sunday-only dress, and caressed it with deep reverence as I set it aside and washed my face with cold water from the well. I dressed myself, then nervously waited to hear the first tolling of the bells, summoning the entire village of Pibrac to worship — including me. "Be good, my dear little lambs," I sung to my flock, who gathered at the barn doors awaiting their routine ramble into the near pasture. "You shall have to wait just a while longer, until I return from church. The bells are calling me!"

I latched the doors to the barn behind me amid the protests of my sheep and sprinted toward the Courbet, glad for the recent dry spell that left stepping stones exposed above the waterline. It would make child's play of crossing the wide, cool stream that could turn into a swift river in a matter of minutes when the flooding spring rains came. In that case, there was also a narrow, wooden footbridge the locals had built, though it tended to wash out under pressure. For now, it stood as a gateway to Paradise. I skipped my way along the greensward on the other side of the Courbet, the tolling of the bells sounding sweet and lovely in my ears. In the near distance, I could see people flocking to the little brick church on the hill, some on foot, others on horseback or in horse-drawn carriages. I could see my own family's carriage, pulled by our dear old mare, Pearl — a grey Percheron whose hips and topline had started to sink due to her advancing age. But she still looked grand and stood out from the dozen or so bay horses and mules common to our village. I watched my father tether her to an iron post and help Hortense down from the sleek, black carriage. It had been my grandfather's carriage and reflected his position as the mayor of Pibrac. It was the one thing my father took care to preserve in all its finery, for he knew he would never be able to afford such a luxury again. While he had inherited the farm and its accouterments, he had not inherited my grandfather's keen business sense or the esteem of the villagers. He had become another peasant farmer among many, although Hortense seemed to think that under her direction, he could restore the House of Cousin to its former glory. It was no wonder then, that a sickly, disfigured child like me didn't fit into her grandiose plans.

Hortense's rotund body, which was draped in a flowing, green chiffon dress, awkwardly spilled out of the carriage, even as she held my father's hand. My stepsisters followed suit, blithely leaping onto the cobblestone and scampering toward the church doors. I watched Jacqueline, clothed in a flouncy yellow dress, deliver a mean, little swat on Pearl's rump as she raced by. I'd seen Pearl kick for lesser offenses. All I can say is that Jacqueline was lucky she was as fast as she was mean. As for me, I moved slowly, quietly, and deliberately in an attempt to attract as little attention to myself as possible. I waited at the end of the walkway for the procession of parishioners to dwindle, then slipped between the crack of the double doors and sank into the shadows of the vestibule. It was from that vantage point that I observed the whole of the Mass, as unobtrusive as a dormouse, just as I had promised. But oh, what a glory it was! I did not understand the whole of what Fr. Michel was saying but there was a stirring — no, a quiet rumble — in my soul. And when Fr. Michel elevated the white circle of bread, my breath quickened and my heart began to pummel my chest. Skin and bones that I was, I was sure one would be able to see it beating beneath my pretty blue dress.

Of course, I came to know that I was meeting my risen Lord, in Person, for the very first time. But in that moment, all I knew was that I was lovely in His sight. It was as though I heard a Voice in my inmost being saying, "Come, child, come to the feast." I was welcome at this table. It would be many months before I would partake of this most holy bread at this most holy banquet, but I never doubted that I had found a place to call home, a place where my hunger and thirst would be forever satisfied.

When Mass was over and Father Michel approached the doors where I hovered nearby with my bruised back pressed to the wall, he cast a sidelong glance at me and smiled. He stopped just short of the threshold and spoke to me tenderly. "Germaine, you must come to Sunday school with the other children. We'll gather in the courtyard behind the church in twenty minutes." He tilted his head at the tears that crept into my eyes. "Don't be afraid, all are welcome here."

"But Father, I haven't permission to attend."

"I will see to that," he said, then leaned down and whispered in my ear. "For now, my child, sit a few feet away from the others. Give them a little time to see how beautiful you are. The Lord will give them eyes to see, I promise you that."

Me? Beautiful? I had felt so at the elevation of the sacred Host, and now I had been told so. In one morning, everything had changed and it was as though the scales had dropped from my own eyes. I was neither my disease, nor my deformity. And although I was stricken by the king's evil, I had already caught a glimpse of the true King whose sovereign touch could heal me. But would he?

The hem of Father Michel's black cassock brushed my bare feet as he swept past me, flung open the doors, and with the vigor of a priest half his age descended the broad, brick stairs of the church known as St. Mary Magdelene. A stream of parishioners poured from the pews and into the central aisle, following his lead. They formed a kaleidoscope of color as everyone bedecked in Sunday finery merged into a swirling pool and the last, fragrant wisps of incense curled in the air above them. It was a heady and harrowing experience for me and I sank back into the shadows when Hortense came into view. My relief at remaining unseen was short lived, for she called out to her daughters in a commanding voice I couldn't help but hear.

"Your father will return for you in one hour. Behave yourselves at Sunday school. Remember, you represent the House of Cousin!"

"Yes, *maman*," Abby dutifully replied, but Jacqueline was too busy arranging the flaxen hair of my doll to pay her mother any mind. I dreaded the thought of being ridiculed by them in front of the other children of Pibrac. But Father Michel himself had called me to attend and I peered out the doorway as he took my father aside. Hortense's face froze into a polite smile that failed to reach her eyes as she monitored the conversation. My father nodded his consent. It was finished.

Several minutes later when the crowd had filtered through, I made my way to the courtyard where children sat beneath the arch of a rustic, fieldstone shrine. In its center was a statue of a beautiful woman draped in a pale blue mantle and crowned with golden stars. I sat with hunched shoulders on a stone wall several feet away, ashamed by the way my bare feet dangled for all the world to see. Father Michel took his place on a wooden stool at the edge of the semi-circle and gave a welcoming nod to me. Jacqueline, who was among the oldest girls in the group, followed the direction of his gaze and dropped her jaw when she saw me. She gathered breath to protest, but Fr. Michel's voice rang out like a sonorous bell.

"Good morning, children of God!"

"Good morning, Father," they answered.

"It is good for us to be here — and to welcome little Germaine Cousin to our classroom today! She will be joining us weekly henceforth, and I know that you will treat her as our sister in Christ, yes?"

The children murmured and looked at me, then each other, with traces of wonder or scandal, depending on their age. I fought the urge to run, to run as fast as I could back to my flock, back to my vine-twig bed, back to a place of refuge from the shame of my appearance, even if it meant suffering pitch on my clothing and ashes on my bread. But

it was too late. I had already seen Beauty and it was calling to my soul
— beauty unto beauty, deep unto deep. I sat taller and straightened
my bony shoulders. I even mustered a smile that made some of the
children turn away in disgust. But my awareness of everyone else in
the courtyard faded as Fr. Michel began to discuss the Gospel we had
just heard in a way that even an unschooled child such as myself could
understand. A few children raised their hands and asked or answered
questions. Others sat idly, lost in their own thoughts or imagination.
Jacqueline continued to play with my beautiful doll's hair, which
had become as tangled as my own. As for me, I felt the first stirrings
of something I later understood to be faith; faith that I was called,
redeemed, beloved, and chosen to be a suffering saint in the eyes of
God, a loving God, who in his time and according to His promise,
would give me, His little shepherdess, a crown of beauty for ashes.

Breathless, I tumbled into the barn and huddled among my flock,
absorbing their fleecy warmth. My pretty, blue dress was sopping wet
and left a trail of water that mingled with my teardrops. I'd been
lulled into a sense of security under Father Michel's watchful eye.
But once class was dismissed and the children dispersed, I was left
to fend for myself. While Jacqueline and Abigail climbed into our
family's grand carriage and were promptly whisked away by my father,
several other children in the village, like me, were left to walk to their
respective homes. That's when the taunts and terrors started. One of
the older boys picked up a rock and threatened to stone me. Another
called me an ogre and began to give chase. A girl about my age curled
her little fingers into monster claws and made horrible screams that

soared above the taunts of others. I ran toward the river as fast as I could, willing to cross it wet if I had to, for I could not outrun the runty mob to the footbridge. And so, blind to the stepping stones, I tumbled headlong into the waters of the Courbet, losing my footing and dragging myself along the riverbed until I reached the other side. I watched one of the older girls shake her fist at me in a warning. If I came back, so would they.

But I had already decided before I had fully crossed the Courbet that I would return to the little brick church on the hill. How could I stay away from the One my heart already loved? From the One who felt like the home I never had? The image of Christ crucified and hanging above the altar had imprinted itself on my soul and gave me a supernatural degree of courage for a seven year old girl. And having dried my tears in Eleanora's wool, I changed into my ragged pink dress, took up my shepherdess staff, and drove the sheep into the near pasture. I didn't bother to grab my tools for spinning, for I understood in a new way that it was a sacred day of rest, dedicated to the Lord. Yes, I would go hungry in the morning owing to my lack of spun wool, perhaps even receive a beating, but I was more concerned with finding favor in the eyes of God.

The sheep spread out to graze in an uneven circle, their woolliness fusing together to give the appearance of a fluffy, white cloud. I perched on a nearby rock and began to speak words that bubbled up from within — my first formal attempts to pray to my Father in heaven. It was a simple prayer I often repeated throughout my life from that day forward, even unto my last breath: *Dear God, please don't let me be too hungry or too thirsty. Help me to please my mother. And help me to please you. Amen.*

Later that summer, I learned to pray to Our Lady in a special way taught to us by Father Michel. At the foot of her statue, he showed us a string of polished black beads upon which he honored and invoked the Virgin Mary while meditating on the life, death, and resurrection of her Son. Soon, we were all praying together, a chorus of children hailing our Mother. I believe it is through that prayer that my classmates — at least the younger ones — began to see me as one of their own, for they started to ignore my deformities and look me in the eyes. A few of them even walked with me to the water's edge after class was over. And before I knew it, they began to cross the Courbet of their own accord, to seek me out on hot summer days in the pasture where I could readily be found spinning wool in a leafy shade. We would gather under a sweet chestnut tree and pray a rosary together as the bells tolled at midday, *Ave Maria!* I was never without my rosary, a length of frayed, knotted baling twine that I fastened around my narrow waist and wore as a spiritual weapon, like a modern-day *Jeanne d'Arc.*

It was after my seventh summer, in the midst of the following lambing season and in time for the great *Dimanche de Pâques* that I received my first Holy Communion from the hands of Father Michel. He offered that first Sacrament privately, knowing that my appearance with the other children receiving the consecrated Host for the first time would give rise to scandal from the parents. From then on, I approached the altar rail on Sundays after everyone else had returned to their pews. The purple lesions around my lips, those pressed to my cheeks, and those presenting as tubular masses on my neck continued to make me an anathema to the congregation, whose repulsion at the sight of me bore holes into my skinny back as I approached the altar. Why they failed to also see the welts and bruises left by Hortense on my spindly arms and legs, or pity my cold, bare feet, is a mystery known only to God. But as for me? The lesions were becoming wounds that marked me as one set apart for suffering, a suffering servant like my

King, whom I never stopped believing would one day save me from those — and even more perilous — evils.

Once I had received the flesh of our risen Lord on my tongue on Sundays, it was all I could do not to abandon my duties at the sound of the bells calling the village to daily Mass. For many years, I yearned to run to the church of St. Mary Magdelene, knowing there were unclaimed graces waiting for me there. I resisted the urge for fear of what might happen to my sheep, having no other shepherd to guard them. Yes, there were shepherd boys in the neighboring fields, but they had already begun to stare at me, as I advanced into my teenage years, with a ravenous look that I can only liken to that of the way I imagine a wolf looks at sheep. And so, I contented myself to obediently care for my flock with the faithfulness and love with which my Savior cared for me, and to imitate His concern for the poor by sharing my meager portion of bread with the beggars I had come to know and love on my way to Mass on Sunday mornings. Not the least of my attention and bread was given to my friend, Pierre, and to the ever-growing circle of young, peasant children who began to seek me almost daily for holy conversation and the recitation of the rosary under a vaulted cathedral of deep blue sky.

Thus, for many seasons, my life was hidden under the stairs and in the green pastures of Pibrac. The Lord continued to instruct me in the school of suffering and under the dome of nature, where I learned to call the stars by name with frosty breath, to salute the sun with my able arm, and to give thanks for every blade of grass for the nourishment it provided to my beloved sheep. Amid my schooling, I continued to spin wool in exchange for bread. Not for me, but for my sisters and brothers who had none at all. The least I could do was share what little I had, knowing that the holy bread I received at the altar had been sacrificed for me. How could I not do the same for my Jesus in the faces of the poor?

So grateful was Pierre for the morsels of bread I shared with him that he gave me a most special gift, one I treasured with my whole heart. He had retained but little memory of his own mother, who passed away when he was an infant. What he did retain, however, and what became his sole and most prized possession, was her kitchen apron. It was made of burlap, as was fitting for the working poor who couldn't afford finer textiles like linen or cotton. But she herself had embroidered a chain of delicate pink posies along the edging, interspersed with golden fleur-de-lis. It was breathtaking in its beauty and simplicity, and my first instinct was to refuse the offering.

"Pierre! You must keep it for yourself, for the sake of your own heart. It has your mother's handiwork on it. It is priceless compared to my crusts of bread!"

"Don't you see, Germaine? You constantly give to me, and to others, from your own want," he argued, stuttering and twitching as he made his case. "But true friends must give — and t-t-take!"

A plea for dignity was in his light blue eyes. I could not refuse and accepted the apron with great honor and fuss. "I shall treasure it, Pierre, all the days of my life! I shall even wear it to my grave!" I said solemnly, as I fastened it around my waist and marveled at its deep pockets.

Pierre grinned. "No need to be dramatic, Germaine. It's just an apron."

I smiled back and giggled. More than anything else, Pierre had, from the beginning, given me the gift of learning to smile amid the toil of days that came and went with little relief. Little did I know then, that very apron would be the cause of a great uproar that would eventually be heard around the world.

4

Springtime was always my favorite time of year. My hands no longer bled from being chapped by the cold and my feet, covered in rags for the winter, were free to frolic over tender grass that sprouted from the warm, moist earth. It was also the most dangerous time of year, when the she-wolves in *La Bouconne* gave birth to their pups and set about hunting for food in the forest with a fierceness that drifted on air and spooked my sheep, even from the relative safety of the near pasture. Five years earlier, when I was twelve and fueled by the zeal of my confirmation, I had fashioned a cross from two large branches and planted it in the ground as a means of protection. Morning and noon, at the tolling of the bells, I would drop my distaff and spindle and lie before it, prostrate in prayer. Afterward, I would rise from the dirt — sometimes even the mud — with never a stain on my clothes or my skin. Occasionally, I fell into a kind of ecstasy that later gave me pause, for I had a duty to my sheep and to my family.

Despite severe beatings from Hortense that continued well into my teenage years, I longed to please my father and my stepmother, and prayed daily for her conversion. I remained extremely slight in build, almost childlike, thin-skinned, and sickly in nature; it did not take much for her hands — or her broom — to bring me to my knees. More than once, she accused me of stealing bread from her kitchen to dispense to the local poor, whom she detested, and then punished me by withholding my rations for several days. She was just as likely to attack me without the least bit of provocation, both on the kitchen doorstep and in the barn, according to her mood. I would offer my back to her as the wounds I received would be less visible — and therefore less scandalous— to the younger children of the village who for a succession of years sought to hear more about our Good Shepherd from the shepherdess of Pibrac. And, in turn, I offered my wounds to Christ in reparation for the sins of the world, knowing that He too had given His back to those who beat Him. Through it all, like my Lord, I remained as silent as a lamb.

Hortense became enraged when a neighbor reported that more and more of the children of Pibrac had taken a genuine liking to me, seeking me in the pasture for spiritual counsel and companionship. The adults in the village and surrounding countryside had taken to calling me "the devout one" with a trace of derision but perhaps not totally without deference. Many parents didn't see the harm, but others forbade their children to approach me. In retaliation for the embarrassment I caused her, Hortense ordered me to take my flock further afield to the pasture that bordered *La Bouconne*, knowing full well the peril that both my sheep and I would encounter there. I feared her nefarious plan was to dispense with me once and for all!

But the Lord had other plans. In fact, no sooner had I obediently driven the flock to the far pasture than the morning church bells began to ring and I felt an irrepressible desire. For many years, I'd made a spiritual pilgrimage in my soul to daily Mass. But that day, I distinctly heard Jesus summoning me and knew that I must go, even if it meant leaving my sheep at the edge of the forest, vulnerable to attack. I felt called to communion in a way I had never been before. I could not deny the divine will of God!

With childlike trust, I thrust my shepherd's staff into the ground like a sword into stone, amazed at my sudden strength and dexterity. I petitioned my guardian angel to keep watch over my sheep and protect them from the ravenous she-wolves. Then I made the sign of the cross over my flock and ran towards the bell tower that loomed in the eastern sky. From that day on, I never missed a day of Mass. Nor did any one of my sheep ever wander off or meet a violent end, for the holy angels of God kept watch in my stead. Day after day, I raced back over the footbridge of the Courbet to find my sweet flock huddled around my staff, calmly awaiting the return of their shepherdess. More than once, Pierre — and some of the neighboring peasant children — bore witness to this holy spectacle and repeated what they saw to anyone who would listen. When word reached Hortense's ears, she vowed to discredit me. How could I ever explain to her that the credit was not owed to me but to the Lord who commands His angels concerning me?

I delighted in my newfound freedom, even though there was often a hard reckoning to be had at Hortense's hands. Come evening, I would gather my paltry crusts of bread and wrap the greater portion of them in my apron to distribute to the beggars in town on my way to morning Mass. "Germaine, you're frailer than we are, keep your bread!" they would implore. But I didn't feel frail. On the contrary, the holy bread I consumed each day made me feel far stronger than my appearance suggested. Sometimes I didn't hunger for any other bread at all! And so, I experienced what I can only call a season of contentment, when nothing could diminish my joy in the Lord. It must have been a palpable joy, for people in the village began to treat me with greater kindness and mercy than ever before. Word even reached my ears that people had begun to cross the Courbet under the cover of night to see if the rumors were true — that the prayers of "the holy shepherdess," who was said to kneel for hours on the dirt floor of the barn in which she slept, often caused marvelous music and mysterious rays of light to emanate from the dilapidated structure. If it is true, I cannot say. I only know that my prayers remained much the same throughout the years and always ended the same way: *Dear God, please don't let me be too hungry or too thirsty. Help me to please my mother. And help me to please you. Amen.*

The spring of my twentieth year followed a winter in Pibrac like no other. We had suffered months of extreme cold and snow, and for the first time I truly wondered if I would survive living in the barn. I hoped my father might think of me with pity, but never once did he venture to check on me or invite me into the house on those most frigid nights. There was no grass to be had in the pastures, which were still covered with more than a foot of snow on the first day of spring. I began to envy my dear sheep who could at least keep themselves warm with the hay that fermented in their bellies. I nearly lost my fingers and toes to frostbite and held back some of the wool I spun to wrap around them like mittens. I knew I would receive even less bread for doing so, but I hadn't a choice. If I didn't survive the winter, neither would my sheep, who had no one to tend to them but me. Pierre brought me a scratchy gray blanket that I suspect he either purchased or donated at great personal cost, for he too looked paler and thinner than he ever had before. One of the well-to-do girls from the village, Jeanne, secretly made her way to the barn and offered me a warm, navy blue woolen cloak that she had outgrown, even through she was several years younger than me. I believe it was her way of honoring the time we had spent together reciting the rosary and speaking of the love of God and neighbor under the leafy boughs of the chestnut trees. Such were the mercies that saved my life that winter, as well as the lives of my sheep, who closed ranks and huddled around me like a blanket of fleece as I slept among them on my vine-twig bed. And such were the mercies that enabled me to cross the frozen Courbet and continue to attend daily Mass, my true sustenance and source of strength.

The first warm temperatures of spring, combined with a tepid, driving rain, led to a snowmelt that inundated parts of Pibrac and the surrounding countryside with fast-moving streams of water. Even this did not deter me from heeding the call of the morning bells, for God had proven trustworthy in all manner of storms. I gathered crusts of bread in my apron that I had squirreled away for a morning such as this and headed toward the Courbet. But it was no longer frozen. It was raging, and the footbridge had already been washed out by fast-moving floes of ice. Jeanne and her younger brother stood on the other side, anticipating my appearance at the usual time. They called out to me amid the din of the falling rain and the roiled waters of the Courbet. Their voices drifted across the chasm, shrill with urgency and concern.

"Germaine, you mustn't try to cross! The water is too high, you will drown!" They flailed their arms over their heads, desperate to be seen and heard. A small crowd began to gather, attracted by the spectacle they created.

"No, no!" other voices chimed in. "Go home, Germaine!"

"You will make Hortese quite happy if you try to cross," another sneered loudly, amused by my predicament.

Suddenly, their voices faded into nothingness and all I could hear was the tolling of the bells. I made the sign of the cross over myself and over the water's edge, then picked up my foot to step forward. It landed firmly on the stony riverbed as angels parted and held back the water so that I might pass through dry-shod. Although my soul basked in wonder and awe, I did not expect anything less. Such was my trust and faith in the God who loved me and called me to communion with Him in the Holy Eucharist. When I stepped onto the bank of the Courbet on the opposite side, I was greeted by a stunned silence. Some looked at me with a new kind of dread not owing to the gross lesions on my face. I later came to understand it was not me they dreaded but the mighty power of God they had just witnessed, the God they suddenly realized was watching them as closely as He was watching me.

From that day forward, the villagers treated me with greater charity. Some adults even offered quiet greetings in the street as I passed by. Gradually, my stepmother's campaign of hate and intolerance began to lose its influence. Though no one yet stepped forward to challenge Hortense, I felt in my bones, which by this time protruded from every angle, that a day of reckoning was coming, not of my own making, but of the Lord's.

5

The late spring and summer of my twenty-first year brought about two momentous events. The first was that Abigail left for Paris, following the footsteps of Jacqueline, who had decided the summer before that Pibrac was far too rustic for her taste — a taste her mother had put into her mouth for finer delicacies in life. Both girls aspired to win the favor of a noble and thereby elevate their social status. There was no such man to be found in the village or countryside of Pibrac, and so Hortense had sent them off — first one, then the other, to claim their rightful place in Parisian society lest they become local spinsters. Before Abigail departed in the prized coach of my grandfather, which was no longer quite so gleaming or grand, she took a moment to peer into the doorway of the barn and call my name.

"Germaine!" she trilled. "You lazy girl! Get up from that wretched bed of yours and come to the doorway! I have something for you."

I stirred as the sheep scattered and vocalized alarm, their white, velvety ears twitching with distrust. It was barely dawn and I was surprised that Abigail would bother to take the time to say goodbye to me, let alone offer a parting gift. I dared to hope it was a loaf of fresh bread or a sweet treat made with local honey that I might share with the beggars of Pibrac. I cast off my blanket and shuffled to the doorway. Abigail inspected me in the pale blue light of morning and pressed her thin lips together in disgust. I instinctively took a step backward, not wanting to offend her by coming too close. She wrinkled her nose at the sight of me and pressed the back of her hand to her nostrils. She had grown taller, thinner, and prettier through the years, but she had lost none of the haughtiness that made her appear miserable and small. Still, I had prayed for her and for Jacqueline without ceasing. They were the only family I had and I wished her well on her journey.

"Good morning, Abby. I hear you're leaving for Paris today. I've been praying for your safe travels."

Abigail sniffed. "Who wouldn't want the prayers of *the devout one*, as the peasants call you," she mocked. "But I know better, Germaine. You're a petty thief who steals bread from the mouths of her family and gives it to beggars and drunkards. I don't know who you think you're fooling, but we are well aware of your duplicity."

I didn't bother to argue. Yes, there were times when Hortense forgot to leave any bread for me for days, or when the cold was such that I longed for just a few more scraps to share with the poor. As I grew older, and bolder, I would sneak into the kitchen seeking whatever crumbs remained for the resident mouse of the House of Cousin. I never took from the warm, fresh bread that Hortense baked, only heels of crust and shards of stale bread that no one else wanted. Those, I would gather in my apron and distribute to Pierre and others on my way to daily Mass. I had no reason to feel ashamed but I did, and turned my face aside.

"I see you're no better for all of your so-called holiness. It seems God has declined to cure the likes of you. Perhaps your weekly confessions are lacking, Germaine, and your soul is no less ugly than your face."

"Perhaps," I allowed, for I myself did not know the mind of God. I could only hope in his mercy.

"Well, then! I've already stayed too long in this dreadful place." She withdrew something wrapped in ribbons and tissue from the folds of her cloak and tossed it on the ground at my feet. It landed with a thud and startled the sheep. "Papa says you're turning twenty-one next week. I thought you might like to have this back. Frankly, it's as used up and pitiful as you are," she declared as she dramatically swirled the fabric of her cloak around her about like a puff of black smoke and departed from my sight. I heard the uneven clopping of Pearl's hooves as the carriage pulled away. She was old and lame and there was not a trace of compassion to be had for her either.

I brushed a stray tear from my eye and picked up the package at my feet. I instinctively knew what was inside before I even unwound the ribbon and peeled back the gay tissue paper. But I was unprepared for the grimness — no, ghoulishness — that had been presented as a birthday gift. With my able hand, I unwrapped my dear Celeste, whose once-beautiful, flaxen hair was was hopelessly knotted and in some places, shorn off. Her dress was in rags. Her immaculate, porcelain face and neck had been discolored to mirror my own disfigurements and her right arm was missing. Her bright blue eyes no longer blinked, but stared into space, looking empty and dulled by the pangs of a slow and tortuous death. Still, I clutched her to my heart and loved her as I did when I was five years old. For her, the reign of terror had come to an end. I hoped and prayed for the blessed day it would end for me as well.

The second event was no less impactful. My dear friend and spiritual guide, Father Michel, passed away that summer at the age of eighty-eight, quite long in years for his generation. I vowed I should never forget the great kindness and consolations he provided, nor the seeds of faith he planted in my soul. I prayed that he would be greeted by angels and the glad words of our Savior in heaven: *Well done, my good and faithful servant!* Though I mourned the loss, I rejoiced at his eternal reward.

In his place was a young priest from Paris whom the villagers were reluctant to embrace. He was citified and seemed ill at ease among the poverty of Pibrac. When he first saw me, his hazel eyes rounded in disbelief, tainted with a trace of horror. I could see him question whether I might be contagious and to be avoided, but I imagine those who had come to know me informed him otherwise. Some spoke to him of angels who watched over my sheep in the pasture near *La Bouconne*, some spoke of the miraculous parting of the Courbet, which happened in the sight of others more than once. Some even spoke of my holiness, though in my own eyes, I was but a lowly shepherdess who loved the Lord. This didn't stop Hortense from drumming up all kinds of accusations against me and hurling them into the ears of anyone who might entertain them. This included polluting the ears of the new priest who was as impressionable as he was young. Or perhaps he was just afraid of the wrath of Hortense and the way she lumbered around town, hunched by the weight of a thousand grudges. As a result, he was little more than polite to me, hurriedly hearing my confessions and mustering a stony face as he placed the Holy Host on my tongue. It was of no consequence to me, for these Sacraments of Love transcend a priest's humanity. What I received, I received from the very lips and flesh and blood of my Lord, my one true hope and consolation!

Nevertheless, with Jacqueline and Abigail gone to Paris, I wondered if my stepmother might have made a bit of room in her heart for me. At the very least, I wondered if my ration of bread might increase, with fewer mouths at the table to feed. And of my father, I thought long and often, wondering if there would ever come a day when he might invite me, his own flesh and blood, back into the house to live with him. For sixteen years, I had lived in the barn and slept on my straw pallet beneath the stairs. I had dutifully and lovingly shepherded my flock of sheep wherever I was assigned — to the near pasture or afar, where my sheep and I were exposed to great harm. I had spun thousands of bundles of wool with gnarled fingers and a useless arm in a spirit of obedience and for a few morsels of food. I had suffered hunger, thirst, and innumerable beatings and abuse at the hands of Hortense and my stepsisters with a fortitude I can only attribute to the power of the Holy Ghost. And for all of this, I only sought to be found pleasing to God and pleasing to my mother. For all of this, my prayer had not changed.

What did change over the years was my blossoming confidence that I had another mother. Not Hortense. Not the one who had given me birth, though I often thought of her, too. But a heavenly Virgin Mother, whose royal mantle was as blue as the summer sky and at whose shrine in the courtyard I often tarried after Mass, offering crowns of wildflowers picked from the banks of the Courbet. It was she whom I hailed at noontime in the pasture, reciting the Angelus on my knees as my flock gathered around me, entering into my rest as I meditated on the mystery of the Incarnation. And it was she whose maternal love seeped into my fingertips as I plied the crude, uneven knots of my rosary and invoked her intercession, *now and at the hour of my death*. I had learned much in the school of the Holy Rosary, not the least of which was that where Jesus is, so is His Mother, faithful to the way of the Cross, faithful to the bitter end, her most pure heart channeling all the graces I needed to reach my heavenly home. Were I to let go of the rosary, I would necessarily let go of her hand. How should I get to heaven without her? And so, my spiritual mother's name — Mary! — was perpetually on my lips.

The amber light of summer slowly yielded to burnished copper, and as all summers do, began to fade away. In a similar way, I knew that I too had begun to fade, my malnourishment and native infirmities taking deeper root and dimming the light in my eyes. Like the falling leaves of the sweet chestnut trees, I began to drop weight, an eighth or a quarter of a pound at a time, until I could count every rib. Raising myself from my straw pallet became a daily hardship. Nevertheless, my first duty was to my flock, to nurture and protect the lambs who had been born that spring and who must learn to know and trust their shepherdess. Once I had collected my bread, I would bask in the red and golden hues of autumn and speak kind words to my flock in the hope that my voice would drift into their ears and settle forever in their hearts. I attended Mass. I shared my bread. I spun more slowly and purposefully, knowing that one day, perhaps soon, I would spin no more.

Pierre sometimes came to sit with me on a golden carpet of leaves. Sometimes we would speak of simple things, such as the changing of the times or the seasons. Other times, we would speak of things that only the afflicted could; the "king's evil" that had stricken me, the impediments of speech and convulsions that bedeviled him. Other times we sat in silence, stunned by the beauty around us. Every now and then, the children would come to visit "the devout one," or "the holy shepherdess" as some of the villagers called me, and we would pray the rosary together or sing hymns of praise. My friend Jeanne, who gave me her cloak years ago, still visited me in the pasture on occasion, though more often she would be the one to courageously break ranks and sit with me in the last pew of the church on Sunday mornings. She didn't much care what Hortense, the new priest, or anyone else thought. I like to believe there's a special place in heaven for those who sit with sinners, tax collectors, and the likes of me.

I remained deeply grateful for that cloak, but especially when the first snowfalls descended on Pibrac. More than ever, I was in need of its thickness and warmth and generous hood to protect me from the elements. I had only the same two dresses to wear, both of them thin and porous, and layered on top by the apron Pierre had given to me. The embroidered pink posies had faded and some hung by threads; the golden fleur-de-lis were no longer as bright as the summer lilies of the field. But the apron retained every stitch of its glory in my eyes, for it had been given in a spirit of unconditional love.

Love. It has supernatural power, does it not? It is love that keeps us alive and love that calls us home. It was also love that compelled me to share my meager bread with those who had none, to gather whatever scraps I could find into that apron to distribute to other beggars like me. That's what I did one cold winter's day, when Hortense was sleeping long into the morning and neglected to leave me any bread at all. I snuck into the house and gathered my portion as well as some scraps, stuffing them into the pockets and folds of my apron before driving my sheep down the road to the far pasture. From there, I planted my shepherd's staff in the frozen ground and left my flock in the care of the angels while I attended morning Mass. I thought it no different than any other morning. But it turned out to be quite different indeed.

No sooner had I crossed the footbridge over the Courbet than I heard a shrill voice carried on the wind at my back. I, as well as a group of villagers milling about the marketplace at the edge of town, turned to face the unpleasant sound. My eyes widened in fear at the sight of Hortense huffing her way toward the footbridge. I had no idea she could move so fast and before I knew it, she was striking at my heels with a thick cudgel in her hand.

"See!" she screeched to everyone and to no one in particular. "See what a wretched, thieving girl your so-called *holy shepherdess* is! Why, her apron is filled with bread she has stolen from my kitchen, bread she did not work for and bread she did not bake! Bread she squanders on the poor while letting her own go without! Go on Germaine," she spat, swatting me several times on my back with the stick. "Show them how holy you are! Open your cloak and show us what you're hiding!"

"Madame Cousin!" some of the villagers protested. "You mustn't treat her so!"

This only served as kindling for my stepmother's wrath. She grew redder in the face and repeated her command while holding her cudgel directly over my head. "Empty your apron!" She pushed me off balance and my cloak spread open. In that moment, I regretted only the waste of bread that would never be fed to the poor once it spilled from my apron. But it wasn't bread that spilled forth. It was an array of magnificent summer flowers instead! I gasped along with the crowd that had gathered. There were dozens of bright pink posies and grand, white lilies with rich, golden centers and several stems of exotic, burgundy roses such as I'd never seen before. They scattered around my feet and infused the frigid air with a heady fragrance, proving their very freshness.

"It is a miracle!" someone shouted. Soon, an even greater crowd pressed upon us proclaiming, *"Nous avons vu un miracle aujourd'hui à Pibrac!"* I myself did not know what to make of it, but the genius of out-of-season flowers that mirrored those stitched on my threadbare apron was not lost on me. In that moment, I understood that God has a poetic sense of justice — and a sense of humor too.

If God laughed, Hortense did not. She scrunched her flushed, puffy face and pitched forward with her hands on her knees, as though she was going to faint. I leaned down and retrieved one of the beautiful lilies from the frosted ground. I offered it to my stepmother who could barely lift her gaze.

"Please accept this flower, Mother. God sends it to you as a sign of his forgiveness." I knew in my heart that it was true, that this event was meant for the conversion of Hortense's soul. The Good Shepherd will go to the ends of the earth to reclaim His lost sheep, the one of ninety-nine who strays from the fold. As a shepherdess, I understand His relentless pursuit and devotion, for I would do likewise for any one of mine.

Hortense tentatively reached out to take the flower from my deformed hand. As her fingers brushed my own, she dropped her cudgel to the ground. The crowd murmured their amazement as the church bells tolled. And I, in haste, went forth.

6

The rest of that winter was milder in both temperature and temperament than other winters that had come and gone. Not only was the wind less bitter than usual, so was Hortense. One evening, not long after the miracle of the flowers, she sent my father to the barn on a surprising errand: to invite me back into the house to live. I didn't know if the villagers or her own conscious had shamed her into making such an offer. I didn't know if her heart had truly experienced the grace of conversion. But I did know and expressed to my father that I could never again accept the comfort of living hearthside while my brethren, the poor and the hungry, languished in the streets. My affiliation, my oneness, was with them. I vowed then and there that I would continue to sleep on my vine-twig bed under the stairs as long as I should live.

"Germaine," my father implored, kneeling at my bedside, "I have been derelict in my duty to you as your father. I should never have permitted Hortense to banish you to this barn. Please forgive me for my horrible neglect ..." His voice broke as it trailed off and my heart was moved with pity.

"Papa, I forgive you! And besides, God has provided all that I needed." I glanced at my flock of sheep who bleated in low tones at the impassioned sound of my voice. "Truly, I love my life as a shepherdess. Yes, I have suffered but I have also been immensely blessed!"

My father buried his head in his hands and subtly swiped a tear from his cheek. He gazed at me intently, without regard for the deformities on my face. "Did I ever tell you that you have your mother's eyes?"

"No, Papa. You never told me."

"She would be very proud of her little girl, of her holy shepherdess."

"I think *maman* would be proud of me for being ... *me*," I countered. "At least that's what I like to think."

"Indeed," my father acknowledged, "there was no limit to her love." He slowly rose to his feet and glanced at our surroundings, taking special note of the gaping holes in the barn boards. "At the very least you will consent to receiving full plates of food, a few more blankets, some decent clothing? Perhaps you could come into the house simply to eat your meals."

"My flock would miss me," I replied, knowing it was true. "But I will accept the food you offer, provided that I may share it with the poor."

"It is yours, to do with as you please," my father conceded. "But you must also eat."

"Yes, Papa," I said.

He leaned down and kissed me lightly on the top of my head and I smiled at him. Not because I felt joy. But because I had learned long ago from my dearest Pierre that mine is the face of Christ in the world.

Before long, there were new lambs on the ground and, no longer required to spend my days spinning wool for bread, I was at leisure to enjoy them and their playful antics in the pasture with a full and contented heart. I'd like to say that my belly was just as full and content, but after so many years of malnourishment, I found it impossible to consume much food without feeling worse for the effort. I preferred to continue to offer my hunger to God and the bounty of my plate to those who had little or nothing to eat. And so, I bundled bread and fruit and sweets that Hortense provided in my apron and brought them with me to Mass each morning to distribute to anyone in need. In one sense, everything had changed. In another, nothing had at all.

I passed those early and late spring days in a spirit of great freedom, but also a spirit of reparation for those who did not know or love the Lord, those who had strayed from the faith, those who were among the lost sheep. I also continued to pray for my stepsisters, who had yet to find husbands in Paris, that they would seek and find the love of God instead. Just before summer, I welcomed them home for a visit with open arms. Well, with one open arm, waving to them gaily despite their obvious lack of enthusiasm for my greeting.

Their first instinct when they saw me outside the barn was to revert to the cruelty with which they were accustomed to treating me. Abigail poked her sister and made a monstrous sound, like she did when I was six. My father sternly informed them that their taunts and indignities toward me would no longer be tolerated. Jacqueline seemed most crushed by the thought while Abigail merely yawned. They both looked to their mother for affirmation. Hortense merely shook her head and quietly bade them to mind their manners. They stayed several days, just long enough to celebrate my twenty-second birthday with a begrudgingly consumed slice of chocolate cake and a glass of champagne. Then my father sent them on their way in a hired coach, for at my bidding, he had formally retired Pearl.

The carnations were starting to bloom by then, and the first wavy fields of grain were showing their golden heads. Lately, I had been feeling especially unwell, with persistent flutters in my chest that felt like a cage full of butterflies! I became easily winded and paced myself as I drove the sheep into the near pasture each day. Fortunately, I was no longer required to drive them into the pasture bordering the forest. I knew the days were over when I could sprint from there to morning Mass as I'd done for many years; in fact, I could no longer sprint at all. But that didn't ever stop me from crossing over the threshold of the church with a spring in my step at the prospect of receiving my true daily bread.

The sheep seemed to sense the change in me. They accommodated my severely shortened stride and my labored, often painful breaths by encircling me tightly as I walked, as though to cushion me should I fall. At night, they drew close to my bedside and chewed their cud and breathed heavy sighs of contentment, somehow knowing they provided great consolation to me. Jesus tells us that none of us knows the hour or the day when we will pass from this life to the next. I only knew that my time was drawing near. How? Because there was a sense of supreme peace that infused my soul amid the increase in my suffering. In truth, I longed for the day when I could say with my Lord: *it is finished.* And He, in his tender mercy, heard my cries.

One mid-June night, unable to sleep and awash in lightly veiled moonlight that seeped through the yawning boards of the barn, I settled into my bed beneath the stairs and began to recite the rosary on my knots of twine. The crickets were singing their midnight song, which offered a soothing, steady rhythm by which to pray. As I closed my eyes and meditated on the Glorious Mysteries, in particular on the descent of the Holy Ghost, I suddenly felt a mighty rush of wind blowing through the barn and my eyes flew open, startled by the sound. My heart seized at the wonder of it all, although the sweet, young lambs surrounding me didn't even stir. It was as if the whirlwind was meant only for me, and I glanced my last glance at the gleaming upper window, even as I clutched my still, sunken chest in awe. There, I saw three virgins descending from the clouds. I closed my eyes and exhaled what little breath remained.

The next thing I knew, I was winding through starlight, ascending toward the shy moon that just moments before had washed over me. My attendants were clothed in flowing, white gowns with garlands of roses upon their heads — a trio of holy virgins ushering me to the throne of my Savior, Jesus Christ. On my own head was a radiant diadem that lit up the night sky, proof that God in his mercy provides a crown of beauty for ashes.

What happened next is not for me to tell, for it is for each man and woman to experience the four last things for themselves. What I can tell you is that very night, I saw the face of God. And He was smiling.

7

M y dear Marié, perhaps you heard the story of what came to pass in the days that followed. News of my death raced throughout the village of Pibrac, for my father, seeing not the familiar sight of me leading the sheep to pasture, and hearing them bleating pitifully in the barn, came looking for me. He found me with my rosary in hand, laying on my vine-twig bed with an expression of joy on my luminous face. He wept over my thin, lifeless body and, later that morning on the fifteenth day of June, called for the undertaker to transport my remains to the church of St. Mary Magdalene.

By then, the entire village had gathered to await my corpse, for speculation of my death had, in fact, preceded my father's discovery. Earlier that morning, there had been two separate accounts given to the young priest of Pibrac by travelers approaching the village just after midnight. Two monks on pilgrimage, coming from Toulouse, had sought refuge from the darkness and the howling beasts of *La Bouconne* as they neared Pibrac. Glancing into the night sky for a better sense of direction, they saw three ethereal virgins dressed in white gowns soaring toward a barn on the outskirts of town that was bathed in a mysterious light. Moments later, amid celestial music, they saw the same three virgins accompanied in the sky by a fourth virgin dressed in white with a shining diadem upon her head. A priest, traveling from the opposite direction at the identical time reported the same spectacle to the parish priest. "It is the holy shepherdess!" the villagers exclaimed. Many of them hastened to the farm where my father confirmed my death and allowed them to witness the angelic light of my face.

"Surely she was a living saint," the locals began to whisper and weep. "Woe to us who did not believe!"

The villagers petitioned the young priest to bury my body with honor beneath the flagstone in front of the altar. After much pressure, he relented, and I was interred in a beautiful, blue satin gown that Hortense herself lovingly chose for me. The children of Pibrac wove a crown of pink carnations interspersed with golden stalks of rye and set it on my head. In my hand, my right hand, which was no longer gnarled, was the candle that had burned during my funeral rites. And my face? In death, it had become nearly as lovely and pristine as the face of Celeste, my beautiful porcelain doll, on the day she was given to me. Only the faintest scars remained.

For forty-three years, my body reposed beneath the flagstone. For some time, it received holy devotion until people began to forget the wonders the Lord had shown through the shepherdess of Pibrac. As villagers were born, died, or moved away, the memory of me faded to black, until one day, a woman of high esteem, who had given generous alms to the church, died in childbirth. The newest pastor of St. Mary Magdalene, one of many over the years, offered her grieving husband the consolation of burying her in a tomb in front of the altar, an offer he gratefully accepted. Imagine the horror — and surprise — when two young grave diggers, with pick axes in hand, penetrated the flagstone and struck an unknown object. With great care, they began to remove the shattered stone, revealing my fragile casket. The tip of the axe had pierced the soft wood and grazed my nose, causing it to bleed. In haste, they summoned the parish priest, who exhumed my body and pronounced it incorrupt. Once more, the villagers flocked to my tomb, wondering who was this angelic young girl dressed in a blue gown with a fresh garland of carnations and rye upon her head? Many speculated, but one knew. My friend Pierre, now well into his eighties, stepped forward and said in a stuttering voice, "It is the holy shepherdess, Germaine. Let me tell you her story."

Thereafter, I was entombed with great dignity above the ground in a glass casket near the pulpit, while my cultus grew and miracles occurred, and the Bishops contemplated what they should make of me. An anomaly? A curiosity? A saint?

That is where you, Marié, first took offense at the sight of my body and held it in little esteem, banishing my incorrupt corpse to the darkest corner of the sacristy. I do not hold it against you, for what was meant for harm, God has once again turned to the good. See? I am truly here, invoked by the devout prayers of your husband. Fear not. As I rest my hand upon your breast, by the grace and will of Almighty God, you and your child are healed.

I should like to continue doing good, as long as the Lord allows. And if you love me at all, dear Marié, in gratitude for my intercession, please God by caring for the poor, sharing your bread, and return with all your heart to the flock of the Good Shepherd, becoming as a little lamb — meek, obedient, and humble of heart.

And if, in a tender moment, you should remember me, remember me with affection as the poor shepherdess of Pibrac. I will hearken to your prayers and work miracles for those who call on my name!

Epilogue

I n an instant, I was cured of my affliction and my holy helper, Germaine Cousin, took flight. The flesh of my breast had returned to normal and my precious infant, René, began to nurse vigorously. By the time my husband returned from the church of St. Mary Magdalene in search of Germaine's intercession, we were both resting peacefully. His eyes, red and swollen with grief, rounded in disbelief. He fell to his knees at my bedside and began to weep tears of relief and thanksgiving.

"How?" was all he could manage to say.

"The Shepherdess," I replied. "We shall provide her with a most fitting tomb so that others may seek her as well."

My husband nodded. Our baby stirred and sighed contentedly. And somewhere up above, in pastures fair and lovely, the saint of Pibrac smiled.

A Prayer to St. Germaine

(St. Germaine Cousin was canonized in 1867)

O St. Germaine, who knows what it is to be abandoned and abused,
forsaken, forgotten, and physically afflicted, who suffered patiently,
with great faith and humility, hear our prayer.

Come, we implore you, to the aid of all who endure abuse and neglect,
the hardship of broken bodies, broken hearts, or broken homes,
and the despair of being unwanted and unseen,
especially those children who suffer the evils of human trafficking.

Give us a heart for the poor, eyes for the lost,
and a spirit of unbound charity.
Increase our hunger for Jesus in the Holy Eucharist.
Help us to bear our afflictions with patience,
trusting God's mercy and love,
knowing that like you, with faith, we can cross the torrents of this life
and arrive safely on the banks of eternity.

Shepherd us, dear St. Germaine,
through this valley of tears, inspiring in us a spirit of joy
and confidence in the treasure and healings that await us in heaven.
And if, by your merit and prayers, we should receive
aid for our intentions *(name them here)*
we offer thanks and praise to God,
and gratitude for your sweet intercession.

Holy Shepherdess, St. Germaine Cousin, pray for us!

(composed by Andie Andrews, © 2023)

About the Author

Andie Andrews is an avid horsewoman, shepherdess, novelist, screen-writer, and blogger who sees the world and writes from a Catholic perspective. She homesteads in Middle Tennessee with her amazing farmhand-husband, a flock of Valais Blacknose sheep (allsaintsval aisblacknosesheep.com), a dozen hens, two sweet, old mares, and a goofy Golden Retriever. When she's not writing, Andie can be found kicking up dust while dancing with horses, tending gardens, chasing chickens, cuddling sheep, mending fences, feeding her family, adoring Jesus, and finding 101 uses for baling twine around the farm.

For more information visit andieandrewsbooks.com

Other Books & Blogs by Andie Andrews

Farming and Homesteading with the Saints (Non-Fiction, Loyola Press); *Ephemeral* - A Novel (Women's Fiction); *Eternal* - A Novel (Contemporary Romance); *Saints in the City* - A Novel (Women's Fiction); *The Legacy of Ruby Sanchez* - A Novel (Christian Historical Romance); *Holy Sheep!* - A blog on faith, our flock, and following the Good Shepherd; and *Christian Cowgirl Poetry* - a blog on all things equine.

For more information and links visit:
https://www.andieandrewsbooks.com

Made in United States
North Haven, CT
28 February 2025

66350655R00040